The
Secret of Cliff Castle

Enid Blyton

Illustrated by
G. Brook

WERNER LAURIE

*Originally written under the
pen-name of " Mary Pollock "*

Re-issued 1951

COPYRIGHT

Contents

Printed and bound by Mackays of Chatham for T. Werner Laurie,
Parkgate, 182 Piccadilly, London, W.1

CHAPTER I

OFF FOR A HOLIDAY

PETER and Pam leaned out of the railway carriage together and waved good-bye to their mother as their train slowly left the long platform.

" Good-bye, Mother !   Good-bye ! "

" Be good ! " called Mother.   " Good-bye !   Have a lovely holiday !   Give my love to Auntie Hetty."

The train went round a corner, and the two children could no longer see their mother. They sank back into their seats and looked at one another, trying to hide their excitement. It was such fun to go off on a holiday alone like this. They had never been a long journey in a train by themselves before.

" I hope Brock will be at the station to meet us," said Peter. " Good old Brock. It will be lovely to see his round, smiling face again."

Brock was their cousin. They were going to stay with him for part of the summer holidays, down in the country village of Rockhurst. Usually they went to the sea, but this summer Mother thought it would be nice for them to be in the country. Then Auntie Hetty had written to invite them for three weeks, and the children had been thrilled.

" We can go to the farm and see all the new animals there," said Pam. " And we can go exploring in the woods and find exciting things there. I hope there are some woods near."

" There are always woods in the country," said Peter. " Anyway, Brock will know all the places to go to. It's fun going to a place we've never been to before ! "

The train sped on. It soon left London behind, and green fields took the place of houses and streets. The train was an express, and stopped at very few stations. The children had sandwiches with them, and when Pam's wrist-watch showed half-past twelve, Peter undid the parcel Mother had handed them, and took out the packets of food.

" I always feel so hungry in a train, somehow," said Pam. " Oooh—ham sandwiches. How lovely ! What's in that other packet, Peter ? "

" Biscuits, and two pieces of cake," said Peter, looking to see. " Oh, and two bars of chocolate as well. What a nice lunch. Mother's put in some lemonade, too—it's in that bag, Pam. Get it down."

Pam reached down the leather bag, in which Mother

8

had squeezed a bottle of lemonade and two cardboard cups. Soon the two children were eating a lovely lunch, watching the scenery as it flew by the carriage window.

"We shall arrive at Rockhurst at half-past three," said Peter. "But we've got to change at Deane. We must look out for that."

It was quite easy to change at Deane. A porter came by, calling, "Change here for Rockhurst! Change here for Rockhurst," and out the children hopped with their suit-cases. The little train for Rockhurst stood on the other side of the platform, and they simply got out of one train and into the other! It was fun.

"Shan't be long now," said Peter. "You know, Pam, I feel awfully excited. I feel as if we're going to have adventures!"

"I feel that too," said Pam. "But I usually do feel like that when I'm setting out on a holiday."

"So do I," said Peter. "But this time I feel we really are. Proper adventures, I mean. Sort of dangerous, you know!"

"Do you really?" said Pam, feeling all excited too. "Oooh, I hope we do have some. I'd like some. School was so dull last term that I could do with something exciting in the hols!"

The train set off, panting and puffing, for it was a small, slow train, drawn by an old-fashioned engine.

"Goodness! Isn't it slow, after the express!" said Pam. "We could almost lean out of the window and pick flowers off the bank!"

Peter laughed. "Well, in another twenty minutes we shall be there," he said. "And then we'll see old Brock."

The time went by, and at exactly half-past three

9

the little train drew in at a small country platform, where red geraniums flared in beds at the back. " Rockhurst ! " shouted the one and only porter. " ROCKHURST ! "

Peter jumped out, and helped Pam down. She looked eagerly up and down the platform, whilst Peter dragged out the two suit-cases and the big leather bag. Pam gave a shriek.

" Oh ! There's Brock ! Brock ! Brock ! Here we are ! Hallo ! "

Brock came rushing up. He was a tall boy, with a strong body, and a red, smiling face. His eyes shone very blue in the sunshine as he greeted his cousins. He was twelve, the same age as Peter, but stronger and taller. Pam was eleven, smaller than either of the boys.

Brock clapped his cousins on the back, and grinned at them. " Hallo ! Glad to see you both ! Welcome to Rockhurst ! "

" Hallo ! " said Peter, smiling. " It's fine to see you, Brock. Golly, you've grown awfully tall since we saw you last year. You make me feel quite small."

" Come on," said Brock, taking one of the suit-cases. " Mother's outside with the pony-cart. It'll just about take us all, though we'll have to put our feet on these cases."

They gave up their tickets, and went out of the station, chattering hard. Pam called out to her aunt, in delight, " Hallo, Aunt Hetty ! Here we are ! It *is* nice of you to come and meet us."

" Hallo, my dears," said their aunt. " Glad to see you. Climb into the cart. Brock, hand up the cases first, and I'll pack them under our feet."

Soon the four of them were driving swiftly along the country lanes. Sally, the pony, was a smart little beast, and cantered along merrily. The sun shone down, and everything looked gay and holiday-like. The children felt very happy.

They soon arrived at Brock's home. It was a comfortable-looking house, rather rambling, set in a nice big garden. The children liked the look of it very much.

" It's a friendly sort of house, isn't it ? " said Pam. " Oh, Aunt Hetty, isn't the beginning of a holiday exciting ? "

" Very exciting ! " said their aunt. " Quite the most exciting part of a holiday, I always think."

" But it isn't going to be the most exciting part of *this* holiday ! " said Peter, as the pony trotted in at the gate and came to a standstill in front of the house. " I've got a funny feeling about this holiday. It's going to be exciting all the way through ! "

" What do you mean ? " asked Brock, in surprise.

" I don't exactly know," said Peter, jumping down, and helping his aunt out. " But I've got a Feeling ! You just wait and see ! "

" Well, I hope your Feeling is right ! " said Brock, and they all went into the house.

CHAPTER II

A LITTLE EXPLORING

TEA was ready when they got indoors. The children washed their hands and brushed their hair. Peter was sharing Brock's little room, and Pam had a tiny room to herself up in the attic. She loved it because it had queer, slanting ceilings, and funny, uneven boards in the floor. She looked out of the window as she brushed her hair, humming a little tune to herself because she was so happy.

The countryside lay smiling in the afternoon sunshine. Cottages clustered together here and there, and cattle grazed in the fields. In the distance, a curious, steep hill caught her eye. It rose up very suddenly, and at the top was a strange building. It looked like a small, square castle, for it had towers at each end.

"I wonder if anyone lives there," thought Pam. "It looks sort of deserted, somehow. I'll ask Brock about it."

Downstairs, round the tea-table, Brock and his cousins chattered nineteen to the dozen about everything, telling each other all their news. Aunt Hetty smiled as she listened, and handed round her plates of home-made scones with jam, and new ginger buns, and currant pasties.

"Anyone would think you hadn't had anything to eat since breakfast-time," she said, as one after another the plates were emptied.

"Well, we did have a good lunch on the train," said Peter, "but it seems ages ago now. I do like these buns, Aunt Hetty. They're the nicest I've ever tasted."

"Shall we go out and explore round a bit, after tea?" said Pam. "I'm longing to. I saw the farm not far off, Brock—and what is that strange sort of castle on the top of that very steep hill towards the west?"

"Oh, that's Cliff Castle," said Brock. "It's called that because it's built on that steep hill, which falls away behind the castle in a kind of cliff."

"Does anyone live there?" asked Peter.

"Not now," said Brock. "Mother, who lived there, years ago?"

"Oh, I don't really know," said Mother. "It belonged to a queer old man who wanted to live quite alone. So he built himself that castle, and lived there with two old servants, as queer as himself. He spent a fortune on the castle. When he died, he left a will which said the castle was to be left exactly as it was, cared for by the two old servants till they died. Then it was to go to some great-nephew, who has never bothered to live there—or even to go and visit the castle, as far as I know."

" Is it really a castle ? " said Pam.

" No, not really," said Aunt Hetty. " But it's built to appear like one, as you see—and I believe the walls are almost as thick as a real old castle's would be. People do say that there are secret passages in it, but I don't believe that. What would a lonely old man want with secret passages ! That's just make-believe."

The children stared out of the window at the lonely castle on the top of the steep hill. It suddenly seemed very mysterious and exciting to them. It stood there, with the sinking sun behind it, and looked rather black and forbidding.

" Is it quite empty then, Aunt Hetty ? " asked Pam.

" Quite," said her aunt. " It must be in a dreadful mess by now, too, I should think, for nobody has dusted it for years, or lighted a fire there to warm the place. The furniture must be mouldy and rotten. Not a nice place to visit at all ! "

Peter and Pam looked at one another. It seemed to them that their aunt was quite wrong. It would be a wonderfully exciting place to visit ! If only they could !

After tea, they spoke to Brock about it. " Brock ! Will you take us to see Cliff Castle one day soon ? To-morrow, perhaps. It does sound so exciting—and it looks so strange and lonely. We'd simply love to explore round about it."

" We'll go to-morrow ! " said Brock. " But come

and see our garden now—and the farm. We've plenty of time."

So the three of them went over Brock's big garden, and admired the vegetables, the outdoor tomatoes, the peaches on the wall, and everything. They saw Brock's exciting play-house in the garden, too, set all by itself out of sight of the house.

" Daddy had this built for me to take my friends to, when we wanted to play by ourselves," said Brock. " You know, Mother doesn't like a lot of noise, and boys can't help being rowdy, can they? So I just take my friends to my play-house when we want a good old game—and we don't disturb Mother a bit! We can play out here on rainy days, too. It will be fun."

Peter and Pam liked Brock's play-house. It was a small, sturdy, little wooden house with a red door, and windows each side. Inside there was one big room, and around it were spread all Brock's possessions—a small gramophone, a big meccano set, boxes and boxes of railway lines, engines, trucks, signals, and other things belonging to a railway—and on a bookshelf were scores of exciting-looking books.

" You *are* lucky, Brock ! " said Peter, looking round. " This is a lovely place."

" Yes—we'll come here and talk when we want to be all by ourselves," said Brock. " Nobody can see us or hear us. It's our own private place."

They went to see the farm, too—and then the sun sank so low that it was time to go back home to supper. The strange castle on the hill showed up clearly as they went down the farm-lane back to their house.

" Brock, do take us to Cliff Castle to-morrow,"

said Peter. " It would really be marvellous fun to explore it. Haven't you ever been there yourself ? "

" I haven't been very near it," said Brock. " I somehow never liked the look of it very much, you know. I think it's got rather a wicked look ! "

" It has, rather," said Peter. " Anyway, do let's go to-morrow ! "

" All right," said Brock. " I shan't mind going with you—though I've never wanted to go alone ! "

It was fun going to bed that night in a strange bed-room. The two boys talked till late, and Brock's mother had to go in twice to stop them. Pam could hear their voices as she lay in bed, and she wished she was with the two boys so that she might hear what they said.

She fell asleep, and did not wake until the house was all in a bustle with its early-morning cleaning. She heard the two boys talking below in loud voices, and she jumped out of bed at once.

" It's holiday-time—and we're at Brock's—and we're going exploring to-day ! " she hummed to herself, as she dressed quickly. She ran downstairs to breakfast feeling very hungry.

" What are you going to do to-day ? " asked Aunt Hetty, pouring out the tea.

" We're going over to Cliff Castle," said Brock. " Can we take sandwiches, Mother, and have a picnic ? "

" All right," said his mother. " You must all make your beds, and tidy your rooms, please, before you go. I'll get you some lunch ready whilst you do that."

It wasn't long after breakfast before the three children were ready to set out. Brock's mother had been very generous with the picnic lunch. She had cut them potted meat sandwiches, tomato sandwiches, and egg sandwiches, and had put some buttered scones, some ginger buns, and some boiled sweets into the packets too.

" There's a tiny shop, not far from Cliff Castle, where you can buy yourselves something to drink," she said. " Here is some money for that. Now—off you go ! "

They set off happily. Brock knew the way, though it was rather a roundabout one, down narrow little lanes, through a small wood, and then across some fields. It was eleven o'clock by the time they got to the little shop where they wanted to buy drinks.

" I'm so thirsty already that I could drink about twelve bottles of lemonade straight off ! " said Peter.

" Well, don't let's drink all of it straight away," said Brock. " The woman here has a well—look, there it is, with the bucket beside it. Let's ask her if we can have a drink of cold water—then we can save up the lemonade ! "

The woman said that of course they could use her well-water. " Have a whole bucketful, if you like ! " she said. But they couldn't quite manage that. They sent down the bucket, and it came up filled with silvery water.

" It's absolutely ice-cold ! " said Pam, gasping a little at the coldness. " But it's simply lovely."

" Where are you off to ? " asked the woman, handing out three small bottles of lemonade.

" To explore round about Cliff Castle," said Peter.

" Oh, I wouldn't do that," said the woman. " Really, I wouldn't. It's a queer place. And people do say that funny lights have been seen there lately. Well, that's very strange, isn't it, in a place that's been empty for years ? "

" Very queer," said Brock, staring at the woman, and feeling rather excited. " What sort of lights ? "

" I don't know," said the woman. " I only know I wouldn't go near that place in the dark, or in the day-time either ! There's always been something queer about it—and there is still ! "

The children said good-bye and went out of the tiny, dark shop. They stared up at the nearby hill, on the top of which stood Cliff Castle. It looked much bigger now that they were near it. It had funny little slit-like windows, just like very old castles had. It certainly was a queer place for anyone to build in days when castles were no longer of any use !

" Well, come on," said Brock, at last. " Don't let's be put off by silly village-stories. Mother says stories always get made up about any deserted place."

" They certainly make it more exciting," said Peter, hitching his kit-bag full of lunch over his other shoulder. " Well—up the hill we go ! "

And up the hill they went. There was no proper road up the steep hill, only a small, narrow path that wound between jutting-out rocks, for it was a very rocky part of the countryside. Stunted bushes grew on the hillside, mostly of gorse. It was exposed to the east winds, and nothing very much grew there.

" Well—here we are ! " said Brock at last. " Cliff Castle ! I wonder what we shall find there ! "

CHAPTER III

CLIFF CASTLE

NOW that the children were right up to the castle, it looked enormous! It rose up in front of them, square and sturdy, a tower at each end. Its small, slit-like windows had no glass in. The great front door was studded with big nails that had gone rusty. There was a large knocker, which the children longed to use—but which, of course, they dared not touch!

"What a lot of steps go up to the front door!" said Peter, standing at the top of the flight, and looking down it. "It must have cost an awful lot of money to build this place. The walls look as thick as can be—made of solid stone!"

" Let's go all the way round the castle and see what we can see," said Pam.

So they went down the great flight of steps again, and began to make their way round the towering walls of the strange castle. It was difficult, because creepers, bushes and weeds grew high up the walls. Tall nettles stood in great patches, and the children had to make their way round them after Pam was badly stung on her bare legs.

" We'll find some dock leaves to help the stings," said Peter, and he found a patch of dark green dock leaves. He picked some and Pam pressed the cool leaves against her burning skin.

" That's better," she said. " Gracious, I shan't go near nettles again to-day ! "

They went on their way round the great grey walls. The slit-like windows were placed at regular intervals. The children gazed up at them.

" You know, in the olden days, they had those funny narrow windows so that archers could shoot their arrows out without being hit themselves," said Brock, rather learnedly. " I can't imagine why the old man should have built windows like that for himself, long after the time of bows and arrows had gone ! It must make the rooms inside awfully dark."

" I wish we could see them, don't you ? " said Pam excitedly. " Just imagine how queer they would look after all these years when nobody has been here— cobwebs all over the place—dust everywhere. Oooh— it would be awfully queer."

They could not go all round the castle, because, when they came to the side that faced due west, the hill fell away so steeply that it was impossible to go any further. The walls of the castle were built almost sheer with the hillside, and there was a very big drop down to the bottom of the hills below.

" Isn't it queer ? " said Brock, peering over the edge of the steep cliff. " I shouldn't care to fall down there ! "

" Let's have our lunch now," said Peter, all at once feeling terribly hungry. " It's almost time. We can find a nice place out of the hot sun and sit down, can't we ? "

" Rather ! " said Brock, feeling hungry too. " Look —what about that shady bit over there, facing the castle ? We can look at the queer castle whilst we're eating."

They sat down in the shady spot, and undid all they had to eat. It had seemed a lot when Brock's mother had packed it up—but it didn't seem nearly so much when three hungry children began to eat it. They unscrewed the tops of the lemonade bottles, and drank eagerly. Except that the lemonade tasted a little warm, it was delicious.

Pam finished her lunch first, because she did not want so much as the boys, and gave some of hers to them to finish up. She lay back against a tree and looked up at the silent grey castle.

She looked at the queer narrow windows and began to count them. When she came to the second row, she spoke out loud :

" Look, Peter ; look, Brock—there's a window in the second row upwards that is bigger than the others. I wonder why."

The boys looked up. Peter screwed up his eyes to see why the window should be bigger.

" I don't think it's meant to be bigger," he said at last. " I think the weather has sort of eaten it away. It looks to me as if the bottom part of it has crumbled away. Perhaps a pipe comes out just there, and has leaked down the window and made the stone and brick-work rotten."

" Do you see the tree that grows up to that window ? " said Brock, in sudden excitement. " I believe we could climb it and look in at that window ! I wonder what we should see if we did ! "

Peter and Pam stared at him, and then at the tree that grew up to the window. What fun it would be if they really could climb it and have a peep inside the castle !

" Well, let's see if we can peep inside any of the lower windows first," said Peter. " I don't think Aunt Hetty would be awfully pleased with us if we climbed trees in these clothes. We really want old clothes for that."

" Oh, bother our clothes ! " said Brock, his red face shining with excitement. " I vote we climb up ! But we'll have a peep in at one of the lower windows first. Peter, you come and give me a leg-up."

It wasn't long before Peter was bending down, heaving Brock up to the narrow window-sill to see inside the slit-like window. Brock peered through, but could see nothing at all.

" It's so dark inside," he said. " It wouldn't be so bad if the sun wasn't so brilliant to-day—but my eyes just simply can't see a thing inside the darkness of the castle."

" Well, we'll climb the tree then ! " cried Pam, running to it. She loved climbing trees as much as the boys did.

" Wait a bit, Pam," cried Brock. " Peter and I will go up first, and give you a hand. You're only a girl, you know."

It always made Pam cross to be told she was only a girl. " I'm as strong as you are, anyway ! " she cried, and looked about for an easy way to climb.

But Brock was up the tree before either of the others. He was a country boy, used to climbing, and he saw at once the best way to go up. He was soon lost to sight among the greenery.

His voice came down to them : " Go up the way I did. It's not difficult."

Peter followed him, and then Pam. Pam had to have a hand from Peter every now and again, and she was glad of it. They were soon all of them up on a high branch beside Brock. He grinned at them.

" Good climbing ! " he said. " Now, look—see this branch ? It reaches right to that window. It's pretty strong, and I think it will bear us all. But we'd better go one at a time, in case it doesn't."

" You go first, then," said Peter. Brock edged his way along the branch, working carefully with his arms and legs. The bough bent beneath his weight and swung down below the window-sill. Brock came back.

" No good," he said. " We'll try the next branch. That looks a good deal stronger—and although it grows right above the window at its tip, our weight will bend it down till it rests almost on the window-sill, I should think."

They all climbed a little higher. Then Brock worked his way along the next branch. As he said, his weight bent it gradually down, and by the time he was at the end of it, its tip rested on the sill itself. Part of it even went right through the window-opening into the castle.

" Fine ! " said Brock. He put one leg across the stone window-sill, and peered into the slit. He could see nothing but darkness. But certainly the weather had worn away the stone around that window, for the opening was almost big enough to take Brock's stout body !

" I believe I could get right inside ! " he called to the others. He stood upright on the sill and tried to work his way in. It was a very tight fit, for Brock was not thin ! He had to squeeze himself in till he almost burst.

He found that the wall was very thick—about a yard thick, before he had got right through the window. Then he jumped down to the floor inside and called out through the slit :

" Come on ! It's not very difficult ! We'll be able to explore the castle from top to bottom, if you can get through ! "

CHAPTER IV

INSIDE THE CASTLE

PAM felt a little nervous about going right into the castle, but she couldn't hold back if the boys thought it was all right. So she followed Peter when he squeezed himself through the slit in the stone walls, and held his hand tightly when he gave it to her to help her to jump down into the darkness.

Two slit-like windows lighted the room they were in. It seemed as dark as night to the children when they first looked round—but their eyes soon grew accustomed to it, and they began to see quite well. Shafts of bright sunlight lighted up the room in two places—the rest seemed rather dark.

They stared round, and then Pam cried out in disappointment :

" Oh—the room is empty ! It's just like a prison cell ! There's absolutely nothing here ! "

She was right. There was nothing to see at all, except for bare walls, bare floor, and bare ceiling. At the far side was a closed door, big and strong. It had an iron handle. Brock went over to it.

" Well, we may be unlucky in this room, finding nothing to see," he said, " but maybe there will be plenty to see somewhere else ! Let's open this door and explore ! "

He pulled at the door by the great iron handle. It opened ! Outside was a dark passage. Brock felt in his pockets, remembering that he had a torch somewhere. He found it, and switched it on.

The passage led from a narrow stone stairway, and seemed to wind round a corner. " Come on," said Brock. " This way ! We'll open a few doors and see what there is to be seen."

He opened a door nearby. But again there was nothing to be seen but bareness. He shut the door, and the noise echoed through the stone castle in a very queer way. It sounded as though dozens of doors were being shut, one after another. Pam shivered.

" Oooh ! " she said. " It's not nice to make a noise in this place. Even a little sound echoes round like thunder."

No room just there had anything in it at all. It was most disappointing. Brock then led the way to the stone staircase. It wound downwards in the heart of the castle, and as it came towards the bottom, grew a little wider.

It ended in a vast room with an enormous fireplace at one end. " This must be the kitchen," said Pam, in surprise. " And I suppose those stairs we came down were the back stairs. There must be a bigger flight somewhere else. I did think they were very narrow stairs for such a huge castle."

The kitchen was furnished. There was a big wooden table, and around it were set stout wooden chairs. Pots and pans hung around the stove. There was an iron pot hanging over what had once been a fire. Brock peered into it. There was an evil-smelling, dark liquid in it.

" Something made by witches ! " he said, in a deep, mournful voice that made Pam jump. Brock laughed. " It's all right," he said. " It's only some soup, or something gone bad after all these years ! "

The kitchen was dark and dirty, and there was not much to be seen there. The children went out of it and came into a great hall from which four doors led off. Brock opened one.

And then, indeed, there was something to be seen ! The big room beyond the door was furnished most magnificently ! Great couches, carved chairs, cabinets, tables—all these stood about the room just as they had been left ! But how mournful they looked, for they were adorned with great spiders' webs, and when the children walked into the room, clouds of fine grey dust flew up from their feet.

Sunlight came in long golden shafts through four of the slit-like windows, and divided the room into quarters. It made the whole room even queerer than it might have been, for the brilliance of the sunlight lay in sharp contrast to the blackness of the shadows in the far corners.

" Oooh ! What an enormous spider ! " said Pam, with a shudder, as a great eight-legged spider ran out from under a table. The boys didn't mind spiders. They didn't even mind walking into the cobwebs that hung here and there from the enormous chandeliers that had once held dozens of candles to light the room. But Pam couldn't bear the strange, light touch of the webs on her hair, and longed to get out into the sunshine again.

" Isn't it queer, to have left everything just like this ? " said Brock wonderingly. " Look at those curtains. They must once have been simply gorgeous—but now they are all faded and dusty."

He touched one—and it fell to pieces in his hand. It was almost as if someone had breathed on it and made it melt !

" The brocade on the furniture is all rotten, too," said Pam, as she felt it. It shredded away under her fingers. " Everything is moth-eaten. What a horrid, sad place this feels. I don't like it. Let's get away."

" No—we'll explore first," said Peter. " Don't be a spoil-sport, Pam. Come with us. You'll be quite all right."

Pam didn't want to be a spoil-sport, so she followed the boys rather unwillingly as they went out of the room and into the next.

The same things were found there—furniture and curtains, rotten and decayed. A musty smell hung over everything. It was most unpleasant. Pam began to feel sick.

" I hate this smell," she said. " and I hate walking into these horrid webs. I can't seem to see them—and it's horrid to get them all round my head."

" Let's go upstairs again," said Brock. " And this time we'll go up by the main stairway—look, that great flight of steps over there—not by the little narrow back staircase we came down."

They mounted the enormous stone steps, and came to some big rooms furnished as bedrooms. Up they went again and came to more rooms. Leading out of one of them was a tiny staircase all on its own. It wound up into one of the stone towers that stood at the end of the castle.

" Let's go up this staircase ! " cried Peter. " We shall get a marvellous view over the countryside ! "

So up they went and came to the open door of a strange, square little room that seemed to be cut right out of the heart of the tower. A tiny slit on each side lighted it. A stone bench ran round the walls, but otherwise there was nothing in the room.

" What a wonderful view ! " cried Pam, peering out of one of the slits. She saw the whole of the countryside to the east lying smiling in the hot August sun. It looked marvellous.

" I can see our house ! " cried Brock. " Over there, beyond the farm. Oh, how tiny it looks ! And how small the cows and horses look, too. Like animals on a toy farm."

So they did. It was fun to peer out and see everything from so high up. But soon the children grew tired of it and thought they would go downstairs again.

So down they went, and then paused on the first floor where they had first squeezed in through the window. But somehow they couldn't find the room they had climbed inside ! It was strange. They opened door after door, but no, there wasn't a tree outside a window.

" I've lost my bearings," said Peter at last. " I've no idea where that room was. Well, if we don't want to stay here all night we've got to get out somehow ! I vote we go right downstairs into the hall, then make our way to the kitchen, and up that back stairway again. We know the room was somewhere near the top of that."

So down they went, into the hall, into the kitchen, and then towards the back stairway.

But just near the stairway was a small door, very low, set in the wall. The children stared at it. They hadn't noticed it before.

" Perhaps we could open this and get out by it," said Peter. " It would save us all that big climb down the tree. I tried the front door to see if we could get out by that, but it was much too heavy. The bolts had all rusted into the door, and I couldn't even turn the handle. Let's try this funny little door."

" It's so low we'll have to bend down to get out of it ! " said Brock with a laugh. They went to the little door and looked at it. It was latched on the inside, but not bolted or locked, though the key stood in the door. Peter lifted the latch.

After a push, the door opened a little way, and then stuck fast. The two boys together pushed hard. It opened just a little further, and sunshine came through.

Peter put his head round the edge. " There's a great patch of nettles and a gorse bush preventing it from opening," he said. " Got a knife, Brock ? I believe if I hacked away at this gorse bush a bit I could make the door open enough to let us out ! "

. . . JUST NEAR THE STAIRWAY WAS A SMALL DOOR . . .

Brock passed him a fierce-looking knife. Peter hacked at the bush, and cut off the pieces that were stopping the door from opening.

" Cut away the nettles, too," begged Pam. " My legs still sting from that other patch we went into."

Peter did his best. Then he and Brock were able to push the door open just enough to let them squeeze through one by one. They were all rather glad to be standing out in the bright sunshine again, after the dim, musty darkness of the silent castle.

" I say—if we just push this door to, and leave it like that, not locked or bolted, we shall be able to get in whenever we want to ! " said Peter. " We might find it rather fun to come and play smugglers or something here. We could pile weeds against the door so that nobody else would notice it."

" Good idea ! " said Brock. So they shut the door gently, then forced the gorse bush back against it, and pulled pieces from a nearby hedge to throw against the door to hide it.

Pam got stung again by the nettles, and almost cried with the pain. Peter had to hunt for dock-leaves again !

" Cheer up ! " he said. " What do a few nettle-stings matter ? We've had quite an adventure this afternoon ! We'll come back here again soon and have a fine time."

Pam wasn't sure she wanted to. But she didn't say so ! The boys talked eagerly about the afternoon's excitement on the way home—and by the time they reached the house, Pam had begun to think that nettle-stings or no nettle-stings, it had all been simply marvellous !

CHAPTER V

IN THE MIDDLE OF THE NIGHT

THE next day Aunt Hetty took Pam and Peter and their cousin Brock in the pony-cart to the sea, which was about three miles away. This was such fun that the three children forgot all about Cliff Castle for a day or two. And then something happened that reminded them of it.

It was something that happened in the middle of the night. Pam woke up and felt very thirsty. She remembered that Aunt Hetty had left a jug of water and a tumbler on the mantelpiece and she got up to get it.

She stood at the window, drinking the water. It was a moonlight night, but the moon kept going

33

behind clouds. It showed up Cliff Castle very clearly, when it shone down. But when it went behind the clouds the castle was just a black mass on the hill.

Then Pam saw something flickering quickly somewhere at the top of the castle. It caught her eye for a second and then disappeared. What could it be?

She stood watching the castle, forgetting to drink the cool water. Then the flicker came again, this time further down the castle. Then it disappeared once more. It came for the third and last time at the bottom.

Pam felt excited. She remembered what the woman at the little shop had said about queer lights being seen in the castle. Now here they were again—and they were real, because Pam had seen them!

" I really must wake the boys and tell them! " she thought. " I know it isn't a dream now—but in the morning I might think it was, and not tell them. But it isn't a dream, I've seen the lights! "

She crept down the stairs and into the open door of the boys' room. They were both sleeping peacefully. Pam shook Peter and he woke up with a jump.

" What is it? " he said loudly, sitting up in bed, surprised to see that it was night.

" Sh! " said Pam. " It's me, Peter. Listen—I got up to get a drink of water—and I saw lights in Cliff Castle! "

" Golly! " said Peter, jumping out of bed and going to the window. " Did you really? I say—let's wake Brock."

But Brock was already awake, disturbed by the noise. He was soon told what the matter was, and went to the window, too. All three watched for a

34

little time—and then, suddenly, a light flickered again, this time at the bottom of the castle.

" There it is ! " said Pam, clutching Peter and making him jump almost out of his skin. " Did you see it ? "

" Of course," said Peter. " And there it is again—on the first floor somewhere this time—and there again, higher up—and now it's right at the very top. Somewhere in that tower, look. It's the very tower we were in the other day ! "

Pam felt a bit frightened. Who could be in the castle so late at night ? The children watched for a little longer and then went back to bed, puzzled and excited.

" I vote we go there to-morrow again, and see if there's anyone there," said Brock. Nothing ever frightened Brock, and nothing ever stopped him from smiling ! He meant to find out the secret of Cliff Castle as soon as possible !

So the next day three excited children met in Brock's play-house in the garden to discuss their plans. They all felt certain that somebody was living in, or visiting, the castle—someone who had no right to be there. Who could it be—and why did he go there ?

" It's no good telling Mother," said Brock. " I'm sure she would laugh and say we were making a fuss about nothing. And, anyway, it would be more fun to go ourselves and solve the mystery."

" When can we go ? " asked Peter eagerly.

" After dinner," said Brock. " We're going over to the market this morning, in the next town. We don't want to miss that. It's fun. Dad will take us in his car."

So it was not until after the three children had been to the market, and had come back and eaten a most enormous dinner that they set off to Cliff Castle once again.

They stopped at the little shop where once before they had bought lemonade. The woman served them again with sweet drinks, which they drank in the shop.

" Any more been heard about the lights in Cliff Castle ? " they asked the woman, when they paid her. She shook her head.

" Not that I know of," she said. " But don't you go wandering about there, my dears. It's a dangerous place."

The children winked at one another. " Don't you worry," said Brock. " We shan't get into any danger."

They went off again, and soon came near the castle, which towered above them on its hill. They climbed the hill by the narrow rocky path and came to the big flight of overgrown stone steps.

" We won't go up the steps, in case there really is somebody in the castle, watching," said Peter. " We'll try and find that tiny little door. You know—the one we left latched."

So they made their way around nettle patches and other weeds until they came to where the little low door was set in the thick stone walls. The branches they had pulled from the nearby hedge were still against it. Nobody had disturbed them.

Each of the children had brought a torch this time. Then they need not keep together quite so much— though, secretly, Pam thought to herself that she would keep very close to Peter !

They pulled at the door, lifting the iron latch as they did so. It opened silently, and the children squeezed through, shutting it after them. They stood in the big kitchen, so dark and musty, shining their torches all around.

There was nothing new to be seen. They crossed the kitchen and went out into the hall—and here Brock gave a cry of surprise, and levelled his torch steadily on something on the ground.

The others looked. Pam couldn't make out why Brock was so excited, because all she saw were footprints crossing and re-crossing the floor—and, after all, they had all walked there themselves last time !

" What's the matter ? " she said.

" Can't you see, silly ? " said Peter, pointing to a set of footprints that went across the floor. " Look at those. Those are not our marks. None of us have feet as big as that, and certainly we don't wear boots studded with nails. You can see the mark the nails have made in the thick dust."

Pam and the others stared at the marks. Yes—it was quite plain that somebody grown-up had walked across that floor. Brock found another track and shone his torch on it.

" *Two* men have been here," he said thoughtfully. " Look—this set of prints shows a narrower foot than the other. Now, I wonder whatever two men were doing here ? "

The children stared at one another. They couldn't imagine why men should visit the castle in the middle of the night. Perhaps they had come to steal something ?

" Let's look in the rooms down here and see if anything has been disturbed," said Brock at last. So they opened the nearest door and looked into the room there, still festooned with cobwebs, and still smelling the same horrid, musty smell.

" Nothing has been moved," said Brock. " And there are only *our* footprints here. No one else's. Let's follow these other prints and see where they go. They show very clearly, don't they ? "

They did show clearly in the thick dust. It was fairly easy to sort them out from the tracks the children themselves had made, for the men's prints were large and had made more impression in the dust. The children followed the prints up the big stairway to the first floor. There, neatly outlined in the dust, was something else !

" Look at that big oblong shape marked in the dust ! " said Brock. " It looks as if someone had put down a big box there, doesn't it ? "

" Yes," said Peter. " And look—there's the mark of another box, or something, further along. It looks as if the men had been carrying something very heavy up the stairs, and had put their load down for a rest before going on. See how their footprints are muddled here, too—as if they had picked up their load again and gone on carrying further along."

" I feel rather like a detective ! " said Pam excitedly. " Tracking things like this ! I wonder where the men took their loads to ! I expect that explains the lights we saw last night. The men had torches, and every time they passed one of those slit-like windows, the reflection shone out for a moment, like a flicker. I guess they didn't know that ! "

" Come on," said Brock impatiently. " Let's follow on."

They went on, past many closed doors and up another flight of stone steps. This brought them to the second floor. The footprints still went on !

" I believe they're going up to that tower ! " said Pam. " We saw the light flicker there, you know. Oh— I hope the men aren't hiding there ! "

This made the boys stop hurriedly. They hadn't thought of that ! Suppose somebody was up there in the tower ? That wouldn't be very pleasant, because they would be sure to be angry to see children interfering.

" We'd better go very quietly indeed, and not speak a word ! " said Brock in a whisper. " Come on."

So in complete silence, their hearts beating fast, the three children crept on and up until they came to the room where the little stone staircase led up into the tower. They mounted it quietly, seeing the men's footprints still on the steps.

They came to the wooden door that had been open the first time they had gone up the staircase. This time it was shut !

CHAPTER VI

A PUZZLE

"IT'S shut!" whispered Brock. "Shall I try and open it?"

"No!" said Pam.

"Yes!" said Peter. Pam clutched Peter's hand. She didn't know what she expected to find behind that closed door, but she felt certain it wouldn't be nice! The boys felt that they really *must* push the door open. They were bursting with curiosity. Brock pushed. It didn't open. He took hold of the iron handle and tried to turn it. It turned—but still the door didn't open.

"It's locked," said Brock at last, in disappointment. "I remember seeing a key here in this big

40

keyhole when we last came here—and now it's gone."

" Look through the keyhole and see if you can see anything," said Peter eagerly. " It's so big that maybe you can."

Brock put his eye to the keyhole. " It's all so dark," he said, " but I believe I can make out shapes of boxes and things. You take a peep, Peter."

So first Peter and then Pam peered through the keyhole, and they both agreed that certainly there were things there that hadn't been there before. They couldn't possibly see if they were boxes or trunks, or what they were, but there *were* things hidden there.

" If only we could get inside and see what's there ! " said Brock longingly. " Something that ought not to be there, I'm sure ! "

The castle was so silent and lonely, and the sound of their whispering voices was so queer, echoing down the stone stairway, that Pam felt nervous again. She pulled at Peter's arm.

" Let's go," she said. " We'll come back another time. Shall we tell anyone about what we know ? "

" I don't think so," said Brock. " It's our own mystery. We've discovered it. Let's try and solve it ourselves. We often read about secrets and mysteries in books—it would be fun to try and keep this one all to ourselves."

They went downstairs again, puzzled to know what was in the tower, and why it was locked. When they got into the hall, Brock switched his torch towards the front door.

" I suppose the men came in at the front," he began— and then, he suddenly stopped. " Look ! " he said, " there are no footsteps leading from the front door.

Isn't that queer ? How did the men get in, then ? "

The three children stared in silence at the enormous door. Certainly the men had not used it. Then which door had they used ? As far as the children knew there was only one other door, and that was the little low one they themselves had used. They felt quite certain that the men had not used the window above, where the tree touched, because it was as much as the three children could do to squeeze inside there. No grown-up could possibly manage it.

" It's funny, isn't it ? " said Peter, at last. " There simply *must* be some other way in."

" Let's follow all the footprints and see where they lead from," said Brock. " If we follow them all, we are sure to come to where the men entered."

So, their torches directed on the ground, the children followed the tracks patiently, one after another. They couldn't understand one lot of tracks at all. They apparently led to, and came from, a room that had once been used as a study. The footprints went in and out of the door—there was a double-track, one going and one coming—and led across the room to the big fireplace, and back again.

" Why did the men come into this room, and out again ? " said Pam, puzzled. " They don't seem to have touched anything here. Why did they come here ? "

" Goodness knows," said Brock, switching off his torch. " Just idle curiosity, or something, I suppose. There doesn't seem anything for them to come for, here. I say—look at the time. We shall be awfully late for tea ! "

" We'd better go, then," said Peter, who, although

42

he wanted his tea, didn't want to leave the mystery unsolved like that. "Come on. We'll come back again soon."

They went into the kitchen and out of the little, low door. They pushed it to behind them, and piled the boughs against it, dragging the gorse bush round again. It hid the door well.

"I hope the men aren't as smart as we are!" said Brock, looking back at the castle. "We've left plenty of footprints there for them to see. They could easily tell that three children have been wandering about."

"I only wish I knew how the men got in and went out," said Peter, still worrying about that. "I feel sure there must be something in that room we last went into to account for their coming and going."

But it wasn't until late that night, when Peter was in bed, that he suddenly thought of something most exciting! Why ever hadn't he thought of it before? He sat up in bed and called Brock's name in such an urgent voice that Brock, half-asleep, woke up in a hurry.

"What's up?" he said. "More lights showing in Cliff Castle?"

"No," said Peter. "But I believe I know how the men got in and out, Brock!"

"You don't!" said Brock.

"Well, listen—you know that often there were secret ways made into and behind rooms through the big chimneys they had in the old days," said Peter. "Well, I believe there must be some kind of way into that room—and that's how the men got into the castle!"

"Crumbs!" said Brock, wide awake now. "I never

thought of that. I wonder if you're right. Maybe there's a secret entrance, then! "

" We'll jolly well go to-morrow and find out ! " said Peter, " even if we all get as black as sweeps exploring that chimney! What ho for a real adventure to-morrow ! "

The two boys told Pam their idea in the morning, and the girl's eyes shone as she listened.

" Gracious! Do you really think there might be a secret way in and out of the castle through that big chimney-place ? It's certainly enormous. I looked up it and it would take two or three men easily ! "

To their great disappointment the children could not go that day to the castle, because Brock's mother had planned a picnic for them. She was surprised when the three children did not seem pleased about it.

" Well ! " she said, " I think you're rather ungrate-ful ! I thought it would be a lovely surprise for you ! "

Pam didn't like to hurt her kind aunt. She went up to her and squeezed her arm. " Of course we'll love to go ! " she said. " We'd planned to do something else—but that can easily wait till another day, can't it, boys ? "

" Oh yes," said Brock and Peter, a little gloomily.

" Well, it can't be anything very important," said Brock's mother. " I'm sure it can wait a little."

So they all went off for a picnic, and they really couldn't help enjoying it, although all three thought longingly of the exciting mystery they hoped they might be able to solve.

Next day the three children set off once more to the castle. They knew the way very well now and took a few short cuts so that it did not take them very long to arrive at the bottom of the hill. They stared up at the great castle, and it seemed to look down on them with a frown.

" Frown all you like ! " said Brock, with a grin. " We'll find out your secret one day ! "

They made their way to the little low door they knew and pulled it open. Into the vast kitchen they went, quite silently. Brock switched on his torch to see if there were any more footsteps to be seen. But there were none. In the hall and up the stairs were the same sets of prints that had been there before—there were no new ones, so far as the children could see.

" The men haven't been here again," said Brock. " Come on—let's go into that room where the prints led to and from the fireplace."

So into it they went, and followed the sets of prints to the big, open chimney-place. This was of stone, and the three children could easily stand upright in it !

" Now, we'll just have a hunt and see if, by any chance, there's a way out of the chimney itself," said Brock, and he switched his torch on to examine the stonework.

" Look ! " cried Pam, pointing to something that ran up one side of the stone chimney. " A little iron ladder ! "

The three of them stared at the little ladder. In the middle of each rung the rust had been worn away a little. " That's where the men went up and down ! " cried Brock. " Come on—up we go ! We're on to something here ! "

45

CHAPTER VII

A STRANGE PASSAGE

BROCK went first up the little iron ladder. Peter
followed, and then Pam. The ladder went up some
way, and then ended.

"It's come to an end!" cried Brock. "But there's
a broad ledge here. I'll give you a hand up, Peter."

He pulled Peter up on to the stone ledge, and then
the two boys pulled Pam up beside them. The ledge
was broad enough to hold all the children quite com-
fortably.

"This funny ledge seems to have been made about
half-way up the chimney, just before it begins to get
very narrow," said Brock, pointing his torch upwards,

46

and showing the others how the chimney suddenly narrowed just above their heads. " We couldn't have gone up much farther, even if there had been a ladder."

" Well, what did the men do ? " said Pam, puzzled. " Surely they didn't just come to this ledge and go back ? "

" Of course not ! " said Brock. " This is where we use our brains a bit. Somewhere round about this ledge is the key to the secret passage that the men used. We've got to find it ! "

" You don't mean a real key that turns, do you ? " asked Pam, looking round and about with her torch, as if she expected to see a large iron key somewhere.

" Of course not," said Brock impatiently. " I don't exactly know what we're looking for, Pam—maybe a lever—or a handle of some sort—or a stone that moves when it's pushed. We just don't know till we try."

So they tried. They hunted for any small bit of iron that might serve as a handle to move a stone. But they could find nothing in the walls around. They pushed against every stone they could reach, but they all seemed as solid as could be. They knocked with their knuckles to see if any stone sounded hollower than the rest, but except for taking the skin off their knuckles, there was no other result !

It was terribly disappointing. The children looked at one another, after about twenty minutes, and wondered what else to do.

" I'm afraid we're beaten," said Peter, at last. " There doesn't seem a thing here that might show us where a secret passage is."

" There's only one place we haven't looked," said Pam suddenly.

The boys stared at her. "We've looked simply everywhere!" said Brock. "You know we have, silly."

"Well, we haven't looked at the stones we're *standing* on!" said Pam. "We've looked at the stonework around and above us—but not beneath our feet!"

"Pam's right!" said Brock excitedly. "Good for you, Pam. You may be only a girl, but you get the right ideas sometimes!"

Pam felt pleased. She only hoped she was right in her idea! The three of them knelt down to examine the stonework under their feet.

It wasn't long before Peter gave a loud cry, which made the others jump. "Look! What's this in this stone?"

They all looked closely, shining their torches down. Set deep in a hole in the rough stone was a sunken iron handle. On the stone by the handle a rough arrow was carved, pointing towards the chimney-hole.

"This is it!" cried Peter. "Brock, what do we do? Pull at the handle?"

"Wait," said Brock. "This arrow means something. See where it points to? Well, I think we have to pull in that direction. Get off the stone, Pam, and Peter and I will see what we can do."

The children's hearts were thumping loudly in excitement. After their disappointment, it seemed too good to be true that they should have hit on something that might show them the way into the secret passage they felt sure was there.

Pam took her foot off the stone, and watched as the two boys took hold of the iron handle and heaved at it in the direction of the arrow. At first nothing happened at all—and then a very strange thing came to pass under their eyes!

As the boys heaved at the handle, the stone in which it was set began to move smoothly outwards as if it were on rollers! It moved towards the chimney-hole, and then, when it seemed as if it really must overbalance and fall down the chimney, it stopped moving. In the space where it had been was a dark hole that led downwards!

"Golly!" said Brock, shining his torch down. "This is exciting, if you like. There's the secret passage, all right! But how do we get down? There's no ladder."

"Look—there's something just a little way down, coiled up on a big staple!" cried Peter, and he shone his torch on it. "It's a rope!"

Brock reached down and pulled it up. It wasn't a rope—it was a rope-ladder. He saw that the top of it was firmly hitched to the staple, and the rest dropped down out of sight. He let go and the rope-ladder swung back to its staple.

"Well, that's the way we go!" said Brock. He shone his torch on to Pam. "What do you feel about it?" he asked. "I know girls aren't so daring as boys. Would you like Peter to take you outside and leave you to wait in the sunshine somewhere, whilst we see where this goes to? It might be a bit dangerous."

"Brock, don't be so mean!" cried Pam indignantly. "I'm not a coward—and do you suppose I want to go away from here just when things are getting really thrilling? I'm coming with you, so that's that."

"Righto," said Brock, grinning. "I thought you would. Don't get all hot and bothered about it. I'll go first. Peter, shine your torch down, old man."

Peter shone his torch down the curious hole, and Brock let himself over the edge and felt about with his feet for the first rung of the rope-ladder. Then down he went, very cautiously. After a bit, he shouted up :

"The ladder has come to an end. There's stone floor here, and a passage leading off. Come on down. Send Pam first, Peter, then you can give her a hand down."

So Pam went next, so thrilled that she could hardly feel for the rungs with her feet ! She went down and down, and at last stood beside Brock, her feet safely on solid floor again. Then came Peter. They shone their torches into the passage that led off to the left of the queer hole.

"This is a real secret passage," said Brock in an excited voice. "A really proper one. Golly—isn't it fun !"

"Come on," said Peter. "Let's see where it leads to. I can hardly hold my torch still, my hand is shaking so !"

They went down the narrow winding stone passage. It was perfectly dry, rather airless, and very small. In places, the children had to bend their heads so as not to knock them against the roof of the passage.

The passage went steeply down, then at intervals turned right back on itself. "It must be made in the walls of the castle itself," said Brock wonderingly. "What a funny thing for anyone to have thought of making. Hallo—what's this ?"

A shaft of daylight had suddenly appeared in one side of the passage ! It came from an iron grille set in the wall of the passage itself.

"THIS IS A REAL SECRET PASSAGE," SAID BROCK IN AN
EXCITED VOICE

" A sort of air-hole, I suppose," said Peter, and he looked out. " I say, do you know where we are ? We are at the west side of the castle—the side that goes sheer down with the steep cliff. I believe there must be a way cut down through the cliff itself, and the entrance to it is somewhere at the bottom of it ! "

" Yes—you're right," said Brock, peering out too. " Well, if that's so, the passage will soon change from a stone one to an earth one—and let's hope it hasn't fallen in anywhere."

" Well, the men used it, didn't they ? " said Peter. " So it must be all right. Come on."

Just as Brock said, the passage soon changed from a stone-walled one to one whose walls were made of earth, strengthened here and there by wood and stones. It zigzagged down, and at the steepest places steps were cut. It was not an easy way to take.

" We must surely be nearly at the bottom ! " said Brock at last. " My legs are getting jolly tired."

There was still a little way to go—and then the secret passage ended abruptly in a small, low cave. The children crept into it, and then out into a larger cave. The entrance to this was set so closely about with gorse and blackberry bushes that it would have been quite impossible to see from the outside.

The children forced their way out, tearing their clothes and scratching their legs.

" You can see where the men got in and out," said Brock. " Just there, where sprays of bramble are broken."

They looked round and about. They were now at the very bottom of the steep side of the cliff, where few people came. It was quite impossible to see the cave from where they stood, although they were only a few feet from it.

"Who would have thought there was a secret way into the very heart of the castle, only a few steps from where we stand," said Brock thoughtfully. "My word, wasn't that a thrill?"

"Do you think we'd better climb back and swing that moving stone back into its place?" said Peter suddenly. "If the men come again, as it's pretty certain they will, they'll see that stone is moved, and suspect someone has been after them."

Brock looked at his watch. "We haven't time to do it," he said in dismay. "Golly, Mother will be angry with us—it's half an hour past dinner-time already!"

"But, Brock—suppose the men see the stone is moved?" said Peter anxiously.

"We'll come back another time and put it into its place," said Brock. "Maybe the men won't be back for some time now. They don't come every night. Come on, now—we'll have to *race* back!"

And race back they did—but it didn't prevent them from being well scolded by Brock's mother!

CHAPTER VIII

BROCK'S ADVENTURE

THE children went to Brock's play-house that afternoon, and talked and talked about their discoveries in the castle. They couldn't say enough about the finding of the strange secret passage. When they remembered that long dark climb downwards through the walls of the castle, and then down the cliff itself, they felt more and more thrilled.

But Peter also went on feeling uncomfortable about the stone in the chimney. He kept saying that the men might come back and discover it.

" Then they'd lay a trap for us and we'd be caught," he said. " As long as they don't know we've discovered any of their secrets we're all right. I do wish we'd had time to put that stone back."

"Perhaps you're right," said Brock, at last. "I'll slip off this evening, after tea, by myself, and put it back. It won't take me long now I know all the short cuts."

"All right," said Peter. But it was not to be, for Brock's mother wanted him to drive the pony-cart over to the farm and collect a crate of chickens for her.

"Oh, Mother! Won't it do to-morrow?" said Brock in dismay. "I've got something I want to do this evening."

"Well, I'm afraid *that* must keep till to-morrow," said his mother. "I've arranged with the farmer to send over for the chickens this evening and he'll have them all ready. Take Peter and Pam with you. It's a nice drive."

So Brock had to go off with his cousins in the pony-cart. "Just after I'd really made up my mind to go and do that at the castle," he grumbled. "I hate changing my plans. I really do feel you're right about that stone now, Peter."

"So do I," said Peter, gloomily. "It would be just our luck if the men came to-night!"

"I'll tell you what I'll do!" said Brock suddenly. "I'll go as soon as we're in bed! It will just be getting dark then, but the moon will be up early to-night, and I'll be able to see my way back beautifully."

"Oooh, Brock! You surely don't want to go to the castle at night-time!" cried Pam in horror. She felt quite nervous enough in the daytime, and she knew she would never be brave enough to go at night!

"Why not?" said Brock with a laugh. "You

don't think I'm frightened, surely ? It would take more than Cliff Castle to make *me* afraid ! ''

"Shall I come with you ? '' said Peter. He didn't really want to, but he felt he ought to make the offer.

"No, thanks," said Brock. "I think it would be best for just one of us to go."

All Brock's family were early bedders, and it was about half-past ten when the boy got cautiously out of bed and began to dress himself. Twilight still hung about the fields, but would soon disappear. Then the moon would come up.

"Good luck, Brock ! '' whispered Peter. "Do you think your father and mother are asleep ? ''

" I don't know," said Brock. " I'm not going to risk going downstairs and opening any of the doors. They are sure to creak ! ''

"Well, how are you going, then ? '' asked Peter in astonishment.

"Down my old apple tree ! '' whispered Brock, and Peter saw the flash of his white teeth as he grinned.

He went to the window and put a leg across. He caught hold of a strong branch, and in a moment had worked his way down it to the trunk. Then down he slid and Peter heard the soft thud of his feet on the ground below. He watched the boy's shadowy figure as he ran down the garden and out into the lane.

" I hope he won't be too long," thought Peter, as he curled up in bed again. " I shall keep awake till he comes back. Then I'll pop up and wake Pam, and she can come down and hear what Brock has to say."

But Peter didn't keep awake. By the time that half-past eleven had struck downstairs, he was fast asleep !

But Brock was wide awake, running like a hare

over the fields. He met nobody, for no one was out so late at night in the country. Grazing sheep lifted their heads to look at him and a startled rabbit skipped out of his way.

Brock saw the moon coming up slowly. It lighted up the castle on the hill, and made it look silvery and unreal.

" It's like a castle out of some old story," thought the boy. " It will be fun to get inside at night-time ! "

Brock was quite fearless. He enjoyed this kind of adventure, and was quite glad to be on his own, without the others to bother about. He ran round to where the little low door was set at the bottom of the castle. He pulled at it and it opened.

He slipped inside. He waited a moment in the great dark kitchen to see if anyone else was about by any chance, but everything was still and silent. The boy switched his torch on, and went into the hall to see if there were any more footprints. But there were none. So the men hadn't yet been—but, after all, it wasn't many hours since Brock had left, and it didn't leave much time for anyone to come.

The boy made his way to the room where the iron ladder led up the chimney. He climbed up the ladder, and soon came to the ledge. The stone that had moved out to disclose the secret passage was still swung out over the chimney-hole. Brock wondered how to get it back.

" I suppose I must heave on the iron handle in the opposite direction," he thought. He took hold of it— and then almost fell down the hole in astonishment. He had heard voices !

" Golly ! " thought the boy, sitting quite still on the

57

ledge, " somebody is coming—two people at least. But where do the voices come from ? "

Brock couldn't distinguish any words, he could only hear the murmur of voices, talking and answering. They came up from the hole, and were getting louder.

" My goodness, someone is coming up through the secret passage ! " thought the boy, in a fright for the moment. " It must be those men. I must get the stone back into place as quickly as I can ! "

With the sound of voices, came other sounds rather like something being bumped against the wall. Brock felt sure the men were carrying something again. He took hold of the iron handle sunk in the stone and heaved hard at it. At first the stone would not move— then, slowly and gradually, it gave way to Brock's stout pulling, and rolled back into its place.

It made a slight grinding noise as it did so, and Brock hoped that the men below were talking loudly enough to drown the sound. He climbed quickly down the iron ladder and ran into the kitchen, meaning to get out of the little low door.

Then he stopped. " No," he said to himself. " This is a big chance for me to find out exactly what the men are up to. I'll hide somewhere, and listen and follow. Golly, what an adventure ! "

He darted behind a big cupboard in the hall, and waited to see what happened. After some while he heard sounds coming from the room he had left. The men were climbing down the iron ladder in the chimney-place, dragging something heavy with them.

Then came the sound of voices, quite clearly, echoing weirdly through the silent castle.

" We ought to be paid double for bringing the goods

up that narrow way!" grumbled one voice. "I'd be willing to risk the front door, but Galli won't hear of it. Come on—we've got to take the things up to the tower now. Then we'll get away quickly. I don't like this wretched moon, showing us up so clearly when we walk outside."

From his hiding-place Brock could see two men, each carrying large and heavy boxes on their shoulders. They were half-bent beneath the weight, and the boy marvelled that they could possibly have carried them all the way up the secret passage, up the rope ladder, and then down the iron one!

"They must be very strong," thought the boy. They were. They had broad shoulders, and when they were caught in a shaft of bright moonlight, Brock saw that they looked rather foreign. He had thought that their voices sounded a little foreign, too. They were very dark and swarthy, and one man wore gold ear-rings in his ears.

They came into the hall, carrying the boxes, and then went up the broad flight of stairs. They put the boxes down for a rest when they came to the top, and again Brock heard the murmur of their voices as they spoke together. The boy crept out from his hiding-place and went to the foot of the stairs.

He followed the men silently up and up until they went into the room from which the little stone staircase led into the tower-room. One of the men unlocked the door at the top. Brock heard them put down their loads and sigh with relief.

"I could do with a drink now," said one man. "Is there a well in the kitchen—or somewhere we can get water?"

59

" We'll look," said the other. He locked the door, and the men came down the narrow staircase again. Brock saw that they had left the key in the door and his eyes gleamed. Maybe he could slip up and take it out before they remembered it—and then he and the others could come and find out what was in those boxes! Something exciting, he was sure !

He slipped out before the men, and ran into one of the nearby rooms. It was furnished, and the boy pulled some curtains around him to hide himself. But the things were quite rotten and fell away as he touched them. Thin grey dust flew all around, and before Brock could stop himself, he sneezed !

CHAPTER IX

BROCK IN TROUBLE

NOW, when Brock sneezed, everyone knew it, for he sneezed heartily and well. In the silence of the castle his sneeze made a most tremendous noise ! It echoed all round and about, and startled poor Brock just as much as it startled the two men.

" There's someone here ! " said one. " In that room. Quick—we'll get him ! "

They darted into the room where Brock had tried to hide. Luckily for him they missed him and he was able to dart out and elude their outstretched hands. He ran down the stairs at top speed, his boots making a tremendous clatter as he went.

The men ran after him. Down and down went Brock, meaning to make for the little low door in the kitchen. But when he got there, it was so dark he could not see where he was going, and he fell over a stool. He crashed to the floor, and had no time to make for the door. Instead, he rolled quickly under a big oak-seat in the fire-place and lay there, hardly daring to breathe. The men switched on their torches, and one of them gave an exclamation.

" Look here—here's a little door, ajar ! "

" That's where the boy came in ! " said the other man. " Well, he didn't have time to get out, that's certain. He's somewhere here. But first I think we'll shut and lock the door. Then our friend won't be able to escape quite so easily as he hoped ! "

Poor Brock heard the door being shut and locked. He felt certain that the man had put the key in his pocket. He couldn't think what to do. He wondered if the men knew of the little back staircase. If he could run up that he might be able to find the room where the big tree touched the window-sill. Then he'd be out in a jiffy and the men couldn't follow him !

" Let's shut the kitchen door, and have a good hunt round," said one man. " He's here somewhere."

Now was Brock's chance. The big kitchen door was at the far end of the kitchen. He stood up quietly, and then made a dash for the little back staircase, which was quite near by. The men gave a shout when they heard him, and switched their torches round to the noise.

" There's a stairway there ! " cried one. " He's gone up. Come on—after him ! "

The men tore up the narrow stairway after Brock.

" If only I could remember which room that tree touched ! " thought the boy desperately. " But we couldn't find it again before. There are so many rooms here, all exactly the same ! "

He ran on till he came to a room and then he darted inside. He took off his boots quickly, because he knew that the noise they made gave him away and made him easy to follow.

The men passed the room, flashing their torches ahead of them. Brock ran to the window. Alas, it was not the right one. It was far too narrow to squeeze out.

Brock ran to the door and peered out. The men had gone to the other end of the stone landing and were looking into each of the rooms as they came back. Brock ran into the one next to his. Again he was disappointed. It was not the right one. He went into a third, his heart beating fast, for the men were now coming back. But again he was unlucky.

He did not dare to go into another room. The only thing he could do was to run back to the staircase and go down it, hoping to hide himself so well somewhere that he would not be found.

As he ran to the staircase the men saw him in a shaft of moonlight and raced after him. Brock almost fell down the stairs, and raced across the kitchen into the hall. Then he tore into one of the big, furnished rooms, meaning to hide behind some furniture.

The men saw him. They went into the room after him, and in a few moments they had found Brock and dragged him out from behind a big dusty couch that smelt so mouldy that the boy was almost sick.

" Well, we've got you now ! " said the man. He shone his torch into Brock's face. " What are you

"WELL, WE'VE GOT YOU NOW!" SAID THE MAN

doing here, spying on us ? You're doing a dangerous thing. We can't let you go, because you've found our secret, and we daren't risk your telling it till we've finished our job and are safe."

Brock said nothing. His red, round face looked surly. The men looked at one another.

" What are we to do with him ? " said one. " He's only a kid. We'd better lock him up somewhere and tell Galli. Then he can put him away till it's safe to let him go. Well, youngster, you'll be sorry for yourself when Galli gets hold of you. He won't be gentle with a nasty little boy who spies on him ! "

Still Brock said nothing. One of the men gave him a shake. " He's lost his tongue," he said to the other. " Come on—let's lock him up in the tower-room with the boxes. He'll be safe there."

So Brock was dragged up to the tower-room, and put there among the big boxes. The men locked the door behind them, and Brock heard their footsteps going down the stairs. He felt sure they would go out by the little low door instead of the difficult way down the secret passage. And they would lock the door behind them, so that Peter and Pam couldn't get in if they came to look for him.

" I've made a mess of things," said Brock, looking at the big boxes. " I wonder what's in those boxes. How I'd like to know ! "

He shone his torch on to one, but soon saw that it was so well fastened and nailed down that it would need strong tools to open it. His bare hands and pocket-knife would be no good at all ! He went to a window and looked out gloomily on the countryside.

A ray of moonlight came through the slit. Far away, Brock could see his own house.

As he looked at it, he saw a light moving in one of the windows. He tried to reckon out which it was, and soon came to the conclusion that it was his own window. Then Peter must be awake. That must have been his torch shining !

In a trice Brock took out his own torch again, and pushed it as far as he could through the slit. He pressed the knob of the torch up and down, up and down, so that it flashed regularly and continually.

" If only Peter sees it, he may guess it's me," thought the boy. " Oh, I do hope he sees it ! I don't want to be kept a prisoner here for days ! "

CHAPTER X

PETER AND PAM TO THE RESCUE!

PETER slept soundly till half-past one. Then he woke up with a jump. He remembered at once that Brock had gone to Cliff Castle, and he sat up in bed to see if the boy was back.

He stared at Brock's empty bed, and then switched on his torch to look at his watch. Half-past one! Whatever could Brock be doing?

As he sat wondering, he heard a sound at the door, and almost jumped out of his skin as a white figure came into the room. It was Pam in her night-dress.

"Peter! Is Brock back? You said you'd come up and wake me when he came back, but it's awfully late."

Peter shone his torch on to Brock's empty bed. Pam felt scared.

"Golly! Where is he?" She went to the window and stared out at the big black mass of Cliff Castle. The moon had gone in for a moment, and it looked very dark and forbidding. Then she suddenly caught sight of a bright little light winking and blinking in the top tower to the right.

"That's funny," she said to Peter. "Look at that light, flashing every other moment, Peter, just as if it were a signal. Those men wouldn't do that, would they, because they wouldn't want to give themselves away. But who else would be signalling like that?"

Peter looked, and as soon as he saw the winking light he guessed that it was Brock. "It's old Brock!" he said. "I'm quite sure it is! What's he doing in the tower-room—it was locked, wasn't it? He must have got in somehow and wants us to go and see what the treasure is in those boxes!"

"Or do you think he's been captured?" said Pam slowly. "He might have been, you know. Maybe he's locked up in the tower."

"We'd better go and see," said Peter, beginning to dress hurriedly. "We won't tell Aunt Hetty, or Uncle, Pam, in case Brock wants us to go and see the treasure with him without anyone knowing. We don't want to give the secret away unless we have to! Hurry and dress now!"

It wasn't long before the two children were climbing down the old apple tree and sliding to the ground below. Then they made their way to Cliff Castle, panting as they ran.

They got there safely, and went to where the little,

68

low door was set in the kitchen wall. Peter pulled at
it, expecting it to open. But it didn't. It remained
tightly shut.

" I say ! It's locked or something ! " he said to Pam.
" Here, help me to pull."

But pulling was no use at all. The little wooden door
wouldn't budge !

" Well, Brock wouldn't have locked it, that's
certain," said Peter, speaking in a whisper. " Someone else must have. I say—I rather think old Brock's
been captured ! "

Pam's heart sank. She didn't feel at all brave and
she was afraid of being captured herself. But somehow
or other Brock had to be rescued, no doubt about that.
This wasn't the time to feel frightened.

" How shall we get in, then ? " she whispered. " Up
that tree ? But, Peter, surely we can't climb it in the
dark."

" We'll have to try," said Peter. " Look, the moon
will be out for some time now—we'll climb whilst it
gives us a bright light. I'll help you. Or would you
rather stay on the ground whilst I climb ? "

" No, I'll climb, too," said Pam bravely. So they
made their way to the tree and Peter shinned up it
first. But Pam couldn't climb it because her legs
trembled so. " I'll just have to stay here," she whispered up to him. " I shall fall if I climb up, Peter.
Isn't it sickening ? "

" Never mind, old girl," said Peter. " You stay
down below and warn me if anyone comes. I'll go in
and see if I can rescue Brock."

Pam couldn't see Peter climbing the tree because it
was full of dark shadows, flecked by moonlight. She

heard the rustling, though, and knew when Peter had reached the bough that led to the window because of the sudden swinging of the tree.

Peter didn't find it so easy to climb the tree in the dark as in the light, but he managed to slide down the branch to the window, and then squeezed himself through. He jumped down on the floor. His boots made a noise, and he took them off. He ran on tiptoe to the door, not making a sound. When he got there he looked out, and suddenly remembered how hard it had been to find that room again. He took one of his boots and made a big cross with it in the dust of the floor. Now he only had to pop his head in at the door to see the cross and know it was the room with the tree outside.

" I feel quite clever ! " said the boy to himself. He ran to the little stone staircase and went lightly down it. The moon was now high and shone in at every slit-like window, so that it was fairly easy to see, though the shadows were as black as could be.

Across the kitchen went the boy, and into the dark hall. Then up the broad flight of stairs on the other side, and on to the first landing. He paused there in the shadows to listen. Was there anyone about ? After all, if Brock had been captured, someone must have captured him—and it was quite likely they might still be somewhere in the castle. This was rather a weird thought, and the boy felt a shiver down his back.

" I won't get into a fright ! " he thought to himself. " I'm rescuing Brock, and I'm not afraid of anything."

He would have liked to whistle to keep his spirits up, but he didn't dare to. As it was, every little sound he made went echoing round and round, and made him jump.

He went on up to the floor where the room was that had the tower staircase leading from it. He came to the stairway, and stood at the bottom, his heart beating so loudly that he felt sure anyone near by could hear it ! He heard a sound from the room above. He stood quite still. Was it Brock there ? Suppose it wasn't ? Suppose it was one of the men waiting to catch him, Peter ? The boy didn't know what to do.

He stole up the staircase, and felt the shut door. He longed to push it open, but he still didn't know if Brock were behind it, or an enemy. And then, suddenly, he knew !

There came the sound of a sigh, and then a creak as if someone had sat down on a box. " Blow my torch ! " said a gloomy voice. " It's no use now—the battery's given out. I can't signal any more."

It was Brock's voice. In delight Peter banged on the door, making poor Brock inside almost jump out of his skin, for he had, of course, no idea at all that Peter was anywhere near. He almost fell off the box.

" Brock ! " came Peter's voice. " I'm here. I'm coming. What's happened ? "

Peter pushed at the door—but alas, it was locked, and wouldn't open. Brock's voice came in excitement from behind the door :

" Peter ! You old brick ! Is the key in the lock ? "

" No," said Peter, switching on his torch. " What a blow ! I can't get in—and you can't get out."

Brock told him shortly how he had been captured. " And now I'm sitting on a box that may contain half the jewels in the kingdom ! " he said. " But I'm a prisoner, and likely to remain one till this man Galli they keep talking about comes along and decides what's to be done with me."

" I'll go back home and get your father to come, and the police," said Peter eagerly. " I don't expect the men will be back to-night."

" Where's Pam ? " said Brock. " Fast asleep in bed, I hope ! "

" No. She's outside the castle, waiting," said Peter. " She couldn't climb the tree in the dark. She said she'd keep watch in case someone came."

" I say, Peter ! I've got an idea ! " said Brock suddenly. " Maybe the other towers have little rooms inside them, with a door like this one. And maybe they all have locks and keys that are the same. Do you think you could go to the tower on this side and see if there's a key in the door of the room there ? If there is, bring it back and try it in this lock—it may fit—and open the door ! "

" Golly ! That's an idea ! " cried Peter, and he went down the staircase and made his way round the big stone landing until he came to the end. He went into the room there and found a staircase leading up to the tower above, exactly like the one in the room he had left. Up he went and came to a door.

" And, my goodness, there *is* a key in the lock ! " said the boy to himself, in delight. He pulled out the key and made his way back. He fitted it into the lock of Brock's door—and it turned ! The lock gave, and the door opened.

" Oh, Peter—what luck ! " said Brock, and he squeezed his cousin's arm. " Thanks, old man—you're a brick to rescue me. Now we must go straight down and join Pam—and then I think we ought to rush home and wake up my father. Someone ought to come and see what's in these boxes!"

Down the little stone staircase went the two boys, both in their stockinged feet. They felt tremendously excited, and Peter's hand shook as he held out his torch to show the way. The mystery of Cliff Castle was nearly solved. The secret was in those boxes. Soon Brock's father would come along and open them. Then, maybe, the two men would be caught and everything would be cleared up.

Just as they reached the first landing they had a terrific shock. A great crashing echoed throughout the whole castle, and the two boys jumped so much that they had to stand still. What in the world could the noise be?

CHAPTER XI

MORE AND MORE EXCITEMENT!

THE enormous crash came again—and then the boys
knew what it was !

"It's somebody banging on that great front-door
knocker ! " cried Peter.

"But who would do that in the middle of the
night ? " said Brock, amazed.

"Pam, of course," said Peter proudly. "She said
she'd watch out—and I expect she's seen someone
coming and that's her way of warning us. What a
marvellous idea ! "

"I say—what a girl she is ! " said Brock admiringly.
"Well—we'll have to look out. Let's slip down to the

kitchen and see if we can get out of that little low door. Maybe the key is on this side."

They ran quietly down the stairs in their stockinged feet—and then paused in horror. In the kitchen, waiting silently, themselves amazed at the noise on the front door, were three men. Two of them Brock had seen before.

The men saw the boys and gave a shout. "Two kids this time!" cried one. "Quick, get them!"

The boys tore into the hall and into the big room where the chimney was that gave on to the secret passage. Brock slammed the door and turned the key in the lock. Then they rushed to the fireplace and climbed quickly up the iron ladder. A heave at the iron ring and the stone moved silently across, showing the way down.

A great noise at the locked door made the boys hurry more than ever. The door would certainly be down very soon, for the lock was sure to be rotten!

It was! It gave way and the door swung open. The three men rushed in and paused. "Surely those kids don't know the secret passage!" cried one of the men in amazement.

"They do!" said another. "Come on—we must get them, somehow, or they'll be away, and tell the police."

They rushed to the fireplace and swarmed up the iron ladder. By this time the boys were at the bottom of the rope ladder, making their way as quickly as they could down the secret stone passage, their hearts beating painfully.

They could hear the men coming after them, and hurried more and more. They came to where the stone passage ended and the earth passage began.

"Hurry, Brock, hurry!" cried Peter. "They are almost on us. Hurry!"

Brock did hurry, but the ground was painful to his stockinged feet. At last the boys came to the small cave and made their way into the larger one. Just as the men got to the small cave the boys forced their way out of the large one, and found themselves on the hillside.

"Up a tree, quick!" whispered Brock. "It's our only chance!"

Peter shinned up a near-by tree, with Brock helping him. Then Brock swung himself up into the dark shadows and both boys lay flat on branches, peering down below, hardly daring to breathe.

It didn't occur to the men that the boys could so quickly have gone up a tree. They thought they had run off into the bushes, and they beat about quickly to find them.

"They'll give it up soon," whispered Brock. He was right. The men soon gave up the search and gathered together. The third man, called Galli, was very angry.

"Fancy letting a couple of kids beat you like this!" he said in disgust. "Now there's only one thing to do—get the stuff out of the tower-room at once and find a new hiding-place. Go on—get back to the castle and haul the stuff out."

The men went off, the other two muttering angrily to themselves, but they were evidently terrified of Galli, who was the leader.

The men went back up the secret passage. As soon as they were safely out of hearing, the boys slid down the tree into the moonlight and looked at one another excitedly.

" Let's get back home as quickly as we can ! " said Peter. " We'll fetch Pam, and run as fast as possible."

" The men will be gone by the time we get Dad and the police here," panted Brock, as they ran up the slope that led to the front of the castle, to find Pam. She saw them coming and jumped out from under a bush.

" Brock ! Peter ! Oh, how glad I am to see you ! Did you hear me crash on the knocker ? I saw the three men coming, and they went in at that little low door. I couldn't *think* how to warn you—and I suddenly thought of that great knocker ! "

" Pam, you're a marvellous girl ! " said Brock, and he threw his arm round his cousin's shoulders and gave her a hug. " Nobody but you would have thought of such an idea ! Honestly, I'm proud of you ! "

The boys quickly told Pam what had happened to them—and then Brock suddenly fell silent. The other two looked at him.

" What is it, Brock ? " asked Peter.

" I've got an idea, but I don't know if it's good or not," said Brock. " Listen—those men are all going back to the tower-room, aren't they ? Well, do you suppose—do you *possibly* suppose we could get there, too, and wait till they're inside—and then lock them in ? "

Peter and Pam stared at Brock. It seemed a mad idea—and yet—suppose, just suppose it could be done !

" The men would never, never guess we were back again," said Peter slowly. " They wouldn't be on the look-out for us. They think we're running off to tell the police. It seems to me that your idea is the only

77

one that might possibly lead to the capture of the men—
and the goods, too ! Otherwise, by the time we get
back here with help, they'll be gone with everything ! "

" We'll try it ! " said Brock. " Now, look here, Pam—
your part in this is to race off by yourself over the
fields and wake Daddy and Mother, and tell them
everything. Will you do that ? "

Pam didn't at all want to do anything of the sort,
but she wasn't going to let the boys down. She nodded
her head. " I'll go," she said, and she went, running
like a little black shadow down the hillside.

" She's a good kid," said Brock, and the two boys
turned to go to the castle. They meant to climb up the
tree and get in that way. They were sure the little
low door would be locked. Up they went and into the
dark room. There, on the floor, was the cross in the
dust that Peter had made !

" Now, quietly ! " whispered Brock, as they went
down the narrow stone staircase. " The men may be
in the kitchen, or the hall."

The boys stole carefully down. There was no one in
the kitchen—and no one in the hall. The boys kept to
the shadows as they walked.

Suddenly they heard a noise, and Peter clutched
Brock by the arm, pulling him into the shadow of a
great hall curtain. " It's the men coming out of the
chimney-place," whispered the boy. " They're only
just back. It's taken them ages to come up by that
steep secret passage. Keep quiet now. We may be able
to do something."

The men clattered across the room to the door and
then went across the hall to the big staircase, talking

in loud voices. It was quite clear that they had no idea at all that the boys were hidden near by. They went up the stairs, and as soon as they had turned a corner, the boys followed them, so full of excitement that they could hardly breathe !

The three men went on up to the tower-room. The boys could hear their voices all the time. They crept after them in their stockinged feet. They had never felt so terribly excited in their lives !

All the men went into the tower-room. Peter and Brock stood at the bottom of the little staircase that wound up to the room, and wondered if this was the right moment to go up.

" Better do it now," said Brock, " or they will start to come out again."

Galli, up above, gave orders to the two men. " Take that box first. And hurry up about it ! "

There came the sounds of two men swinging a box round to get hold of it.

" *Now !* " whispered Brock, and the two boys shot up the stairs, one behind the other, breathing fast. They got to the door. The men hadn't heard a sound. By the light of their torches Brock could see two of them lifting one of the boxes, whilst Galli stood by. The boy caught hold of the wooden door, and closed it as quietly as he could. But it made a slight click as the latch went into place. At once Galli noticed it and roared out a warning.

" Look out ! There's somebody on the stairs ! " He rushed to the door. But Brock had already turned the key in the lock.

Galli hammered on the door in a rage and the stout door shook under his blows.

" Hammer all you like ! " shouted Brock, exultingly. " You're caught ! "

The boys turned to go down the stairs—and then Peter's sharp ears caught something that one of the men said.

" I've got a key to this door ! I took it out of the lock when I shut up that kid. Here, take it, Galli, and undo the door. We'll catch those boys if we have to hunt the castle from top to bottom ! "

Peter clutched Brock by the arm. " Did you hear that? They've got the key to this door, Brock ! The one that was in the door when they locked you up ! Now what are we to do ? "

Brock dashed up the stairs again. He switched his torch on to the door, at the same moment as he heard a key being put into the lock from the other side. His torch showed him a big bolt at the top of the door and another at the bottom. Hoping and praying that they would not be too rusty to push into place, the boy took hold of the bottom bolt. He pulled at it, but it stuck badly.

Meantime the men on the other side of the door were trying to turn the key to unlock it. But it was more difficult to do that from inside than outside. Muttering a string of foreign-sounding words, Galli tried to force the key round.

" Let me try the bolt, Brock," whispered Peter, and took Brock's place. But it was no use. He could only move it a little way, it was so rusty.

" Try the top one," said Brock. So Peter stood on tiptoe and tried the one at the top. He was trembling from head to foot, for it was terrible to hear someone doing his best to unlock the door from the inside, whilst he, Peter, was trying with all his might to bolt it from the outside !

" Oh Peter, Peter, won't it move ? " groaned Brock, feeling certain that they would be captured if the door was unlocked. Peter suddenly gave a shout, and there was a creaking sound. The rust on the bolt had given way and the bolt had slid slowly into place. The door was bolted !

Almost at the same moment the key turned on the other side and unlocked the door—but it was held by the bolt, and Galli roared with rage as he found that the door would not budge. It gave at the bottom, but the stout bolt at the top held firmly.

The boys were both shaking. They had to sit down on the stairs and lean against one another. Neither boy could have gone down the stairs at that moment. They sat there, close to each other, and heard the three men losing their tempers with one another. They shouted in a strange language, and at times one of them would shake the door with all his strength.

" I hope that top bolt holds," said Peter in a whisper. " Everything in this house is so rotten and old that I wouldn't be surprised if the wretched thing gives way."

" Well, let's try to use the bottom bolt as well then, when the men leave the door alone for a moment," whispered back Brock. " Come on—there's a chance now."

The boys, both together, tried to move the bottom bolt back into place. Peter took Brock's knife and scraped away the rust as best he could. Then they tried again—and to their great joy and relief, the bolt slowly and haltingly slipped into place. Now the door was held at top and bottom, and the boys felt pretty certain that the men could not possibly get out, even if they tried all their strength together on the door.

The men did try once more—and this time they found, of course, that it would not move at the bottom.

" They've fastened the door at the bottom, too, now ! " shouted Galli, and the angry man struck the door with his fists, and kicked at it viciously with his foot.

" Hope he hurts himself ! " whispered Brock, who was feeling much better now. He had stopped shaking, and was grinning to himself to think how neatly all the men were boxed up together. " I say, Peter—I rather think we've done a good night's work ! "

" I rather think we have, too ! " said Peter, and the two boys hugged themselves as they thought of all they had gone through to catch the men.

" I hope Pam gets home safely," said Brock. " I wonder how long it will be before she brings help back. Some time, I expect, because Dad will have to get in touch with the police. Well—I'm quite content to wait here till somebody arrives. I guess we're feeling a bit more comfortable than those three men ! "

CHAPTER XII

THE SECRET COMES OUT !

MEANTIME Pam was speeding across the fields and along the shadowy lanes. Once she had started she no longer felt afraid. She had to bring help to the boys, and that help rested on her swift·feet. " Quick, quick ! " she kept saying. " I must run like the wind ! "

And run like the wind she did. She came to her aunt's house at last, and hammered on the front door, for she did not want to waste time by climbing in at the window. Her uncle awoke at once and came to his window. When he saw Pam standing there in the moonlight he thought he must be dreaming.

" Uncle ! Uncle ! Let me in, quick ! " cried Pam.

" There isn't a moment to be lost ! The boys are in danger ! "

In two minutes Pam was inside the house, sitting on her uncle's knee, pouring out the whole story to him as quickly as she could. He and his wife listened in the utmost amazement. Aunt Hetty could hardly believe the story, but Pam's uncle did at once, and saw that he must act quickly.

" I'll hear all the rest later," he said to the excited little girl. " If those two boys have managed to capture the men as they planned, we must go there at once—and if they haven't managed to, they'll be in the gravest danger. I'll ring up the police now. Hetty, see to Pam. She'd better go back to bed."

But nothing in the world would have persuaded Pam to go back to bed that night ! " I'll climb out of the window if you make me go to bed ! " she cried. " Oh, Aunt Hetty, I *must* go back to Cliff Castle. I must, I must ! "

And, as it turned out, she did, because when her uncle came back from the telephone he said that the police wanted her to go with them to take them to the right room. It wasn't long before a police car roared up to the house with four stout policemen inside !

Pam and her uncle squeezed into the car too, and they set off to Cliff Castle by the road. It was a much longer way than across the fields, but it didn't take very long in the powerful police car.

" Why, look at that light in the sky ! " said Pam suddenly, pointing to the east. " What is it, Uncle ? "

" It's the dawn coming ! " said her uncle, with a laugh. " The night is going. Hasn't it been a long enough night for you, Pam ? "

" Yes, it has," said Pam, suddenly feeling glad that the daylight would soon be there. " I wonder how we can get into the castle, Uncle ? There are four ways in— but three of them are almost impossible."

" What are the four ways, Missy ? " asked the inspector, who was sitting beside her.

" There's the front door," said Pam, " but the locks and bolts are all rusted, and we couldn't open it. Then there's a little low door set in the foot of the castle by the kitchen—but that's shut and locked. And there's a secret passage from the bottom of the steep cliff, through the walls of the castle, and up a chimney."

" My word ! " said the inspector, startled. " How ever did you find out all this ? I must say you children are pretty daring ! What's the fourth way in ? "

" It's the way we used first," said Pam. " Up a tree and in at a window. But I'm afraid you're all too big to squeeze in there ! "

" We'll break in at the little low door ! " said the inspector with a chuckle. And that is exactly what they did do !

The two boys were still sitting together on the stairs, feeling rather sleepy, watching the dawn put silver fingers in at the slits of window, when they suddenly heard the noise of the police car roaring up to the castle. Then they heard loud blows on the little door far below.

" They're breaking in ! " cried Brock, in excitement, and he jumped to his feet, almost falling down the stairway. " They're knocking down that little door. Now they're in—golly, they're here ! Pam ! Pam ! Here we are ! "

Pam came tearing up the big staircase, followed by her uncle and the four policemen. She rushed into the room off which the little winding stairway led up to the tower-room, shouting as she came.

" Peter ! Brock ! Did you manage to catch the men ? Uncle's here and four policemen ! "

" Yes, we've got the men ! " shouted Brock, and grinned as he saw Pam's excited face coming round a bend in the stairway. " We've bolted them in well and truly ! "

The men had fallen silent when they heard the shouts. They knew perfectly well that everything was up, as far as they were concerned.

" Get away down the stairs, you three children," commanded the inspector, suddenly taking on a new and quite stern voice. The children badly wanted to be in at the finish—but they didn't dare to say a word. They had to go and wait in the room below whilst the police unbolted the door and rushed the three men.

There was a lot of yelling and struggling, but the five men against the three were too strong, and it wasn't long before a sorry procession came down the winding stairway in charge of three policemen.

" Take them into a room and stay with them till I come," ordered the inspector. Then he beckoned to the three children.

" Come along," he said, " we're going to open those boxes. You deserve to see what's inside, since it was you who really captured the men ! "

In the greatest excitement, the children followed the inspector and Brock's father upstairs into the tower-room. The great boxes lay there, still unopened.

The inspector had the right tools with him and began

to force open the boxes quickly. They were very well fastened indeed, and even when the clasps had been forced back, the ropes cut, and the iron bands severed, there were still the locks to open. But the inspector had marvellous keys for these. " One of these keys will open the locks," he told the watching children. " It's my boast that I've got keys to open any lock in the world ! "

The locks of the first box clicked. The inspector threw back the heavy lid. What looked like cotton-wool lay on the top. Pam pulled it aside.

Then everyone cried out in astonishment and awe— for lying in the box were the most marvellous jewels that the children had ever seen or heard of. Great red rubies shone and glowed in necklaces and tiaras. Brilliant green emeralds winked, and diamonds blazed in the light of the torches that shone down on the jewels.

" I say ! " said Brock's father, finding his tongue first. " I say—inspector, these are not ordinary jewels. They are worth a fortune—many fortunes ! What are they ? "

" Well, it looks to me as if they are the private jewellery of the Princess of Larreeanah," said the inspector. " They were stolen on the steamer, when she fled from her palace in India to this country. It's an amazing story. She had them all put into these boxes and safely fastened in many ways. They were put into the stronghold of the steamer she took. They were apparently guarded night and day—and were taken ashore with her when she landed in this country. But when the boxes were opened at her bank in London, they contained nothing but stones ! "

... THE MOST MARVELLOUS JEWELS THAT THE CHILDREN
HAD EVER SEEN ...

" But how could that be ? " said Pam, her eyes opening wide in amazement. " And how are they here, then ? "

" Well, I suppose what happened was that one of the guards on the steamer was bribed by some clever thief who knew what was contained in the boxes," said the inspector. " He must have had boxes of exactly the same size and make all ready, filled with stones— probably hidden inside big trunks of his own. At the right moment he must have got into the place where these boxes were stored, exchanged them, and then put these boxes into his own big trunks, and gone ashore safely with them."

" And the poor Princess went off with the boxes of stones ! " cried Brock. " Was it that man Galli, do you think ? "

" Yes, I should think so," said the inspector, beginning to open another box. " He's very like a famous thief, one of the cleverest we have ever come up against, whom we already want for another daring robbery. He's shaved off his moustache and beard, but I noticed that he had a little finger missing—and so has this thief I was telling you about ! My word—look at this ! "

The second box was now open, and contained just as amazing treasures as the first. Pam took out a wonderful tiara, rather like a small crown, and put it on.

" Now you're worth about fifty thousand pounds ! " said her uncle. " Do you feel grand and important ? "

" Oh, very ! " said Pam, with a laugh.

" Well, you've every right to feel like that," said the inspector, shutting the first box and locking it. " But not because you're wearing famous jewels. You can feel grand and important because you and your brother and cousin have made it possible for us to recover all this jewellery and to catch the thieves who stole it ! At the moment I should say you are the most daring and clever children in the whole of the kingdom ! ''

Even Brock blushed at this. All the children felt pleased.

" Well, it didn't seem very clever or daring whilst we were doing it," said Peter honestly. " As a matter of fact, I kept feeling frightened—and I know poor old Pam did."

" It's braver to do a thing if you feel afraid than it is to do it if you don't mind," said the inspector. " I don't know what to do with these boxes. I think I'll handcuff those three men together, send them off in charge of two of my men, and leave the third man here on guard whilst I go and report to Scotland Yard."

" What's Scotland Yard ? " said Pam in surprise.

" It's the place where all the head-policemen work !" said the inspector, with a sudden grin. " Very important place, too ! Well—come along. You children must be tired out."

They went down the stairs. The inspector gave his orders, and the three sullen thieves were handcuffed together, so that two policemen could easily take charge of them. The third one was sent up to guard the tower-room.

" I'll send back a car for Galli and the others," said the inspector. " I'll take these children home, and then their uncle can come along with me to the station."

Pam almost fell asleep in the car. She was completely tired out. But the two boys were still excited.

They looked out of the car windows at the sun just rising in the eastern sky. It seemed ages and ages since yesterday! Could so much have possibly happened in one night?

Brock's mother made all the children go to bed when they got back. " You look absolutely worn out," she said. " Tell me everything when you wake, Pam. I'll undress you. You are falling asleep as you stand ! "

The boys were glad to get into bed now, though it seemed odd to go to bed when the sun was just rising. Brock snuggled down.

" Well, good-night," he said to Peter. " I mean, good-morning ! What adventures we've had. I'm sorry they're over. I did enjoy solving the mystery of Cliff Castle."

" Yes, we soon found out the secret," said Peter. " But, oh—I'm sorry it's all ended ! "

But it hadn't quite ended ! The Princess of Larreeanah was so overjoyed at the recovery of her jewels that she came herself to see the three adventurous children.

She arrived in a magnificent car, and was wearing some of the jewels. Much to the children's embarrassment, she kissed them all !

They didn't like being kissed by strangers, even if this stranger was a Princess—and they made up their minds they weren't going to like her. But they soon changed that idea when they found what she had brought for them in a small van that followed her car !

" Open the door of the van and see what is inside for you ! " she said to the three surprised children. Brock pulled open the doors at the back of the van—and all three stared in amazement and awe at the Princess's wonderful present.

91

"It's a car—a small car just big enough to take the three of us!" said Brock, staring at the marvellous little car inside the van. It was bright red, with yellow bands and yellow spokes to the wheels. The lamps, wind-screen, and handles shone like silver.

"It goes by electricity," said the Princess. "I had it made especially for you. You don't have to have a driving-licence, of course, because it is listed as a toy car. But actually it is driven just like a real one, has a horn and everything, and goes by electricity, so that you don't need petrol."

"Let's go for a ride in it now!" shouted Peter in excitement. So they pulled out the magnificent little car and got into it. Brock drove it. He pulled a lever, took hold of the steering-wheel, and off went the car down the lane with its three excited passengers.

"What a wonderful end to an adventure!" cried Peter. "Didn't I say we'd have real, proper adventures? And wasn't I right?"

Well—he certainly was!

THE END